DRAGONBLOOD

THE MISSING FANG

BY MICHAEL DAHL

ILLUSTRATED BY
FEDERICO PIATTI

STONE ARCH BOOKS
a capstone imprint

Zone Books are published by
Stone Arch Books
A Capstone Imprint
151 Good Counsel Drive, P.O. Box 669
Mankato, Minnesota 56002
www.capstonepub.com

Library of Congress Cataloging-in-Publication Data is
available on the Library of Congress website.

Library binding: 978-1-4342-1923-7

Art Director: Kay Fraser
Graphic Designer: Hilary Wacholz
Production Specialist: Michelle Biedscheid

6/10

TABLE OF CONTENTS

Introduction

A new Age of Dragons is about to begin. The **powerful** creatures will return to rule the **world** once more, but this time will be different. This time, they will have allies. Who will **help** them? Around the world, some young humans are making a strange discovery. They are learning that they were born with **dragon blood** — blood that gives them **amazing powers**.

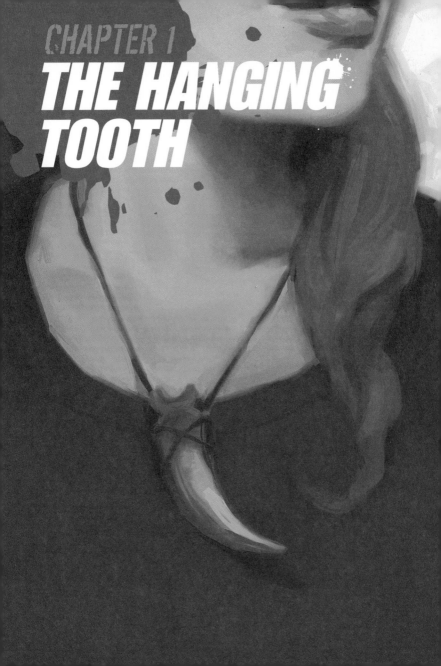

CHAPTER 1
THE HANGING TOOTH

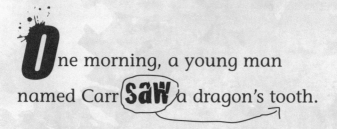

One morning, a young man named Carr **saw** a dragon's tooth.

Carr was a scientist at a college in Scotland.

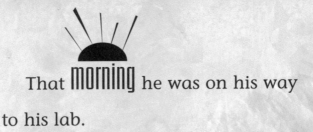

That **morning** he was on his way to his lab.

Carr saw a young woman wearing a necklace. A **STRANGE**, curved stone hung below her neck.

"Excuse me," said Carr. "I like your **NECKLACE**."

"Oh, thanks," said the young woman.

"May I ask where you got that?" Carr asked.

? ?

The woman laughed. "My boyfriend made it," she explained.

She held it out for Carr to get a better look.

"He found the stone on **Snair Island**," she said.

"He was there with some friends on a vacation."

The young woman smiled and then **hurried** away to class.

Carr stood there, amazed.

He had **recognized** the stone hanging from the necklace.

It was NOT a stone. It was a tooth. A **DRAGON'S** tooth.

CHAPTER 2
SNAIR ISLAND

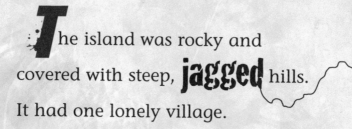

The island was rocky and covered with steep, **jagged** hills. It had one lonely village.

Carr visited the village shops and talked with people.

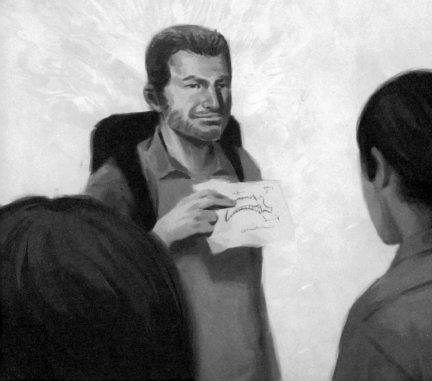

He showed them a drawing of the dragon tooth.

"Have you seen anything like this?" Carr asked them.

The village people shook their heads.

They did **NOT** understand what Carr was talking about.

Finally, Carr visited a small, **DUSTY** bookstore.

The owner listened carefully to Carr and nodded his bald head.

"Yes, I have seen a stone like that before," he said. "Many of them. You can find them up in the hills."

Carr thanked the old man and left the bookstore.

Through his window, the owner
watched Carr walk down the street.

There was FEAR in the old
man's eyes.

CHAPTER 3
THE STONE HUT

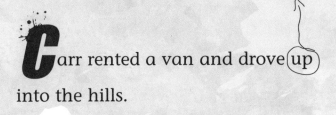

Carr rented a van and drove up into the hills.

The road was **rough** and full of holes.

Hour later, **high** in the hills, the road ended.

Carr had to get out and **walk**.

The sun was **beginning** to set when Carr saw a small stone hut.

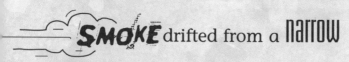 **SMOKE** drifted from a narrow chimney.

Carr knocked at the **wooden** door. A boy opened it. He looked ～ surprised. ～

"Come in," said the boy.

In the hut's main room was a
fireplace.

A thin, red-haired woman sat
warming herself by the **fire**.

Carr **explained** that he was a scientist.

He had come to **Snair Island** to study the rocks.

Then he showed them a picture of the dragon tooth.

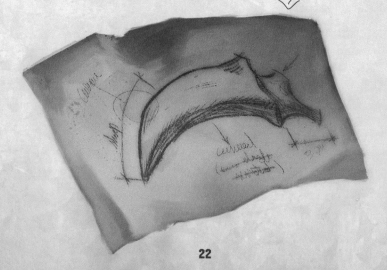

The boy's eyes grew **wide**.

He looked at the woman and then back at Carr. The woman nodded.

"Yes," she said. "Jamie can show you tomorrow."

Then she and the boy **invited** Carr to eat with them. They did not have much food, but they gave Carr the **BIGGEST** helping.

That **night**, the woman and Jamie slept in front of the fire.

They gave Carr the hut's **only** bed to sleep in. He slept in a tiny room behind the fireplace.

It was **midnight** when a noise woke Carr. He looked out the bedroom's small window.

Outside, above the trees, flew a giant **shadow** with wings.

Then Carr saw another, smaller shadow. It flew **somersaults** in the starry sky.

The **HUGE** wings flapped and beat against the air. The scientist smiled.

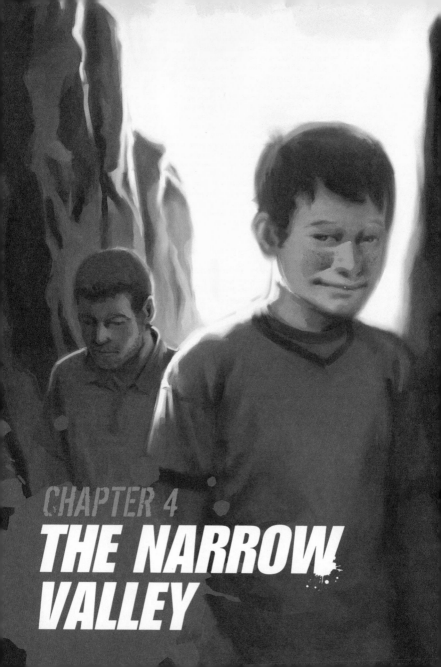

CHAPTER 4
THE NARROW VALLEY

The next morning, Jamie led Carr higher into the hills.

They came to a **DARK**, narrow valley. Smooth cliffs rose on either side.

The boy seemed to be searching the **ground**.

Carr began to **stare** at the ground too.

"**Here!**" shouted Jamie.

He was holding (something) in his hand.

A **tooth!**

"Yes," said Carr, excited. "This is what I was hoping to find."

Carr noticed **BLOOD** on the end of the tooth.

This is **fresh**, he thought.

Carr smiled and looked down at Jamie.

The boy smiled back.

One of his teeth was missing.

FANG FACTS

Most children start losing their teeth around 6 or 7 years of age. They often place the lost tooth under a pillow for the tooth fairy. Centuries ago, there were other ways to dispose of a lost tooth.

* In England, many mothers burned the teeth. This prevented a witch from getting the tooth and using it to place a curse on the child.

* Ancient Egyptians would throw the teeth toward the sun.

* In Europe, parents would bury the tooth. They did this for two reasons: to ensure the growth of a new tooth, and to protect the children from witches.

* VIKINGS gave children a tooth fee in exchange for their baby teeth.

Today people wear **shark** tooth necklaces for fashion. But men in Hawaii have worn them since early times to protect them from evil.

An average person has **32** teeth — eight incisors, four canines, twelve molars, and eight pre-molars.

The **enamel** on your teeth is the hardest thing in your body. It is even harder than bone.

Teeth start **growing** six months before birth.

One in every 2,000 babies is born with a tooth already **showing**.

ABOUT THE AUTHOR

Michael Dahl is the author of more than 200 books for children and young adults. He has won the AEP Distinguished Achievement Award three times for his nonfiction. His Finnegan Zwake mystery series was shortlisted twice by the Anthony and Agatha awards. He has also written the Library of Doom series. He is a featured speaker at conferences around the country on graphic novels and high-interest books for boys.

ABOUT THE ILLUSTRATOR

After getting a graphic design degree and working as a designer for a couple of years, Federico Piatti realized he was spending way too much time drawing and painting, and too much money on art books and comics, so his path took a turn toward illustration. He currently works creating imagery for books and games, mostly in the fantasy and horror genres. Argentinian by birth, he now lives in Madrid, Spain, with his wife, who is also an illustrator.

GLOSSARY

chimney (CHIM-nee)—an upright pipe that carries smoke out of a house

hut (HUHT)—a small, primitive house

jagged (JAG-id)—uneven and sharp

lab (LAB)—short for laboratory, a room containing special equipment for people to use in experiments

narrow (NA-roh)—not broad or wide

recognize (REK-uhg-nize)—to see and understand something

rough (RUHF)—not smooth

scientist (SYE-uhnn-tist)—a person who studies nature and the physical world

somersault (SUHM-ur-sawlt)—tucking one's head into one's chest and rolling in a complete circle

steep (STEEP)—sharply sloping up or down

valley (VAL-ee)—an area of low ground between hills

DISCUSSION QUESTIONS

1. Why did **Carr** want one of the dragon teeth?

2. What do you think about Jamie and his mom? Were they good **people** or bad? Talk about your answer.

3. Where did the **TOOTH** come from that Jamie gave to Carr?

WRITING PROMPTS

1. Imagine that you are a **young** dragon. Write a letter to a friend describing the adventures you have.

2. In this book, Jamie lives with his mother. **Choose** one of the people you live with to write about. What is that person like?

3. What do you think **happens** after this book ends? Write a chapter that extends the story.